POEMS FOR
JEWISH HOLIDAYS

SELECTED BY

Myra Cohn Livingston

ILLUSTRATED BY

Lloyd Bloom

Holiday House / New York

FOR

Alan Marcus Jacobus

January 4, 1954 — August 4, 1975

M.C.L.

Text copyright © 1986 by Myra Cohn Livingston
Illustrations copyright © 1986 by Lloyd Bloom
All rights reserved
Printed in the United States of America

Library of Congress Cataloging-in-Publication Data
Main entry under title:

Poems for Jewish holidays.

SUMMARY: A collection of sixteen poems, by twelve
contemporary authors, celebrating Jewish holidays such
as Yom Kippur and Purim.
    1. American poetry—Jewish authors.   2. Fasts and
feasts—Judaism—Juvenile poetry.   3. American poetry—
20th century.   4. Children's poetry, American.   [1. Fasts
and feasts—Judaism—Poetry.   2. American poetry—
Collections]   I. Livingston, Myra Cohn.   II. Bloom,
Lloyd, ill.
PS591.J4P6   1986   811′.54′08033   85-27179
ISBN 0-8234-0606-7

CONTENTS

It is a tree of life
for those who cleave to it

עֵץ חַיִּים הִיא
לַמַּחֲזִיקִים בָּהּ

4

HOLY DAYS

Suddenly, in the
Midst of everything
New—paved cities,
Calm suburban
Gardens, endless
Acres of corn—

There rise these
Palms, these deserts,
These bitter herbs:
These ancient days
Called up by the
Ram's echoing horn.

Valerie Worth

ROSH HA-SHANAH EVE

Stale moon, climb down.
Clear the sky.
Get out of town.
Good-bye.

Fresh moon, arise.
Throw a glow.
Shine a surprise.
Hello

New Year, amen.
Now we begin:
Teach me to be a new me.

Harry Philip

HOW TO GET THROUGH THE MEMORIAL SERVICE

If restless, let little words
come to your aid:
drop an "e" into "fast"
and enjoy the sudden feast.
Double the "o" in God.
That's good.
Count the burnt-out bulbs
drooping from the high ceiling.
Each dark bulb is a teardrop
among the living lights.

If restless still,
peek at your mother.
See the teardrops wet her cheek
like melted snow.
Someone she softly misses:
her big sister, your aunt,
who cried these very prayers
last Yom Kippur.
Now touch your mother's hand.
Let her feel your light.

Richard J. Margolis

SUKKOT

Here, where
we build our sukkah,
the air is sweet:
  Fragrant earth, our floor.

Here we
lay green bough and pine
to lace our roof:
  Sun shines through, and stars.

Here we
hang festoons of grape,
apple and pear:
  Fruits of late summer.

Here we
heap pumpkin and squash,
tall sheaves of corn:
  Gifts of autumn fields.

Here we
summon Abraham
and our fathers:
  Ancestors of old.

Here we
welcome in Sarah
and our mothers:
  All are exalted guests.

Here we
invite the hungry
to share our food:
  Let them enter in.

Winding
palm branch with willow
and green myrtle
  We weave our lulav.

Citron,
fragrantly scented
is our etrog:
  We wave it in prayer.

Here we
remember our past
and our people
  Who lived by the land.

Here we
will give thanks to God
for earth's bounty:
  Thanksgiving is ours.

R.H. Marks

SIMHAT TORAH

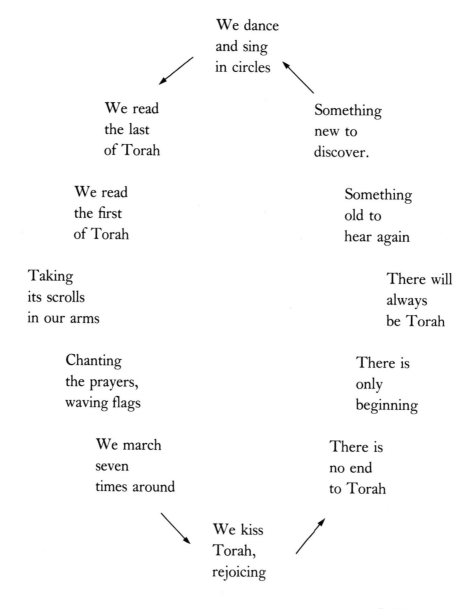

We dance
and sing
in circles

Something
new to
discover.

We read
the last
of Torah

Something
old to
hear again

We read
the first
of Torah

There will
always
be Torah

Taking
its scrolls
in our arms

There is
only
beginning

Chanting
the prayers,
waving flags

There is
no end
to Torah

We march
seven
times around

We kiss
Torah,
rejoicing

R.H. Marks

DREIDL

Hanukkah, Hanukkah,
One for the kitty! The
Four-sided spinner has
Already spun,

Promising plenty of
Pennies to winners—it's
Wobbling, toppling
Over YOU'VE WON!
J. Patrick Lewis

FIRST NIGHT OF HANUKKAH

I shouldn't tell you this, BUT
sometimes we fight! Why does Julie
get to light the shammash candle
every time?

Josh grabs the shield we painted
blue and white—he says he's ALWAYS
Judah Maccabee because
he's oldest. (We can be the brothers.)

NOT FAIR!
I'm the one who found the dreidls
for our game. I'm the one who knows
the names on all four sides—
   NES GADOL HAYAH SHAM

Sunset now. December's early
dark. No one remembers what we
quarreled about—or why. We love
each other in the shining light
of one brave candle.

Mother's the one who looks around and says,
"A MIRACLE HAS HAPPENED HERE
TONIGHT."

      Ruth Roston

TU BI-SHEVAT

Here
our saplings
will send young roots
deep into earth;

Next year,
fresh shoots
will leaf and blossom
over our land;

Here
with a song of joy
we stand

in this New Year of Trees,
in our green time of year.

We are ready to plant!
We are here! We are here!

Myra Cohn Livingston

15

THE FOURTEENTH DAY OF ADAR

See the spring sky
full of kites and small birds!

Our kitchen
fragrant
with honey and poppyseed
fills up with fat little
three-cornered pies—*Hamantaschen!*

Tonight
in my long dress I will be
Esther the Queen.
Tonight
on a small stage I will save
my people. I will remember
my lines.

"There he crawls!" I will say
to the King.
"There he crawls—in his
three-cornered hat—the serpent, Haman!"

Come into our Purim kitchen
and nibble the three-cornered
hats—sweet to recall
a sweet queen, a sweet victory,
a wicked man   gone!

Barbara Juster Esbensen

AN ONLY KID

An only kid! An only kid!
My father bought for two zuzim *had gadya.*

Then came the cat
And ate the kid
My father bought for two zuzim *had gadya.*

Then came the dog
And bit the cat
That ate the kid
My father bought for two zuzim *had gadya.*

Then came the stick
And beat the dog
That bit the cat
That ate the kid
My father bought for two zuzim *had gadya.*

Then came the fire
And burned the stick
That beat the dog
That bit the cat
That ate the kid
My father bought for two zuzim *had gadya.*

Then came the water
And quenched the fire
That burned the stick
That beat the dog
That bit the cat
That ate the kid
My father bought for two zuzim *had gadya.*

Then came the ox
And drank the water
That quenched the fire
That burned the stick
That beat the dog
That bit the cat
That ate the kid
My father bought for two zuzim *had gadya.*

Then came the butcher
And killed the ox
That drank the water
That quenched the fire
That burned the stick
That beat the dog
That bit the cat
That ate the kid
My father bought for two zuzim *had gadya.*

Then came the angel of death
And slew the butcher
That killed the ox
That drank the water
That quenched the fire
That burned the stick
That beat the dog
That bit the cat
That ate the kid
My father bought for two zuzim *had gadya.*

Then came the Holy One, blessed be He,
And destroyed the angel of death
That slew the butcher
That killed the ox
That drank the water
That quenched the fire
That burned the stick
That beat the dog
That bit the cat
That ate the kid
My father bought for two zuzim *had gadya.*

from the *Haggadah*

21

from PASSOVER 1970

Pharaoh's horses were closing in behind us.
We shouted and dodged in the dark, stumbling down to the beach,
shoving aside even our fathers and children,
trampled, half-drowning, cursing our foolish escape from Egypt,
when Moses said:

> Stand still, my people. I must think what to do.
> Stand still. I will not let you perish.
> O Lord, you created the earth
> and the water that covers the earth—
> how can I, a mere man,
> separate the sea,
> reverse your plan,
> and give my people a safe path
> to the other side?
>
> Help me.

And the waters parted. We walked, astonished, on a dry path
as the waves lifted up and froze on either side.
Not a drop of water touched us.
When we reached the other shore we looked back:
our enemies were thrashing about in the waves,
their shields, armor, lances tossing
as the turbulent waters closed over their heads
and swallowed up every rider and horse.

When we saw we were safe, we began to sing and dance,
shouting Hallelujah, and thanks and praise to the Lord.

Ruth Whitman

YOM HA-AZMA'UT

Hanging their harps upon the willows
       our fathers and mothers sang:

      If I forget thee, O Jerusalem,
      let my right hand forget her cunning.

      If I do not remember thee
      let my tongue cleave
      to the roof of my mouth
      if I prefer not Jerusalem
      above my chief joy.

Taking their harps from the willows
       our fathers and mothers sing again.

                    Meyer Hahn

SHAVUOT—FOR JESSICA

Now that it is May, the sky stays light
An hour after supper. Usually I play
Outside. Instead, I climb to the attic tonight.
Closed off from lilacs and sleepy bird songs, I brush away

Dust from a leather trunk. Inside, I find
A faded photo of Grandfather when he was a boy just my size,
Dressed in a strange old-fashioned way. His eyes look kind.
He looks like me. And, then, to my surprise,

He speaks: "Today is Shavuot, the sixth of Sivan.
On this, the Feast of Weeks, Jews celebrate the end
Of the ancient spring harvest and that morning, when
At Mount Sinai, God told Moses to ascend

To receive the Torah." I ask, "What do you mean?"
Then I become the boy in the photo, wearing old-fashioned clothes.
My mother and sisters fill the house with green
Branches and flowers. Father and my older brothers

Leave for the study house to chant all night until dawn.
I want to, too, but I'm too young. I yawn.

In the morning, my whole family goes to pray.
The synagogue floor is strewn with grass.
I stand next to Father. We are on top of Mount Sinai.
We wait to receive the Torah from God, along with all other Jews.

The rabbi takes the Torah from the Ark. It wears
A flower crown! We hear the story of Ruth, so loyal
That she followed Naomi back to the Jews, to share
In her fate. She said, "Your people shall be my people,

And your God my God." Ruth became the grandmother
Of King David. The prophets say
That from King David's children's children's children
The Messiah himself shall come one day.

After the service, we go home to eat
A feast of blintzes and cheesecake,
Because the Torah is like milk and honey, mild and sweet.
Shavuot is the day of happy give and take.

In the dust, once again, I hear my mother's voice
Small as a feather, calling me to bed.
I tiptoe downstairs. I hold a lily of the valley in my fingers
And sweetness in my head.

                                        Kathryn Hellerstein

TISHAH BE-AV

Destroying Jerusalem, burning Solomon's Temple,
Nebuchadnezzar, King of Babylon, returns:

Sacking the city, setting afire the second Temple,
Titus and his Roman legions return:

Strong enough to uproot the Cedars of Lebanon,
Bar Kokhba and his brave heroes return:

> Hadrian, receiving the head of Bar Kokhba;
> Nebuzaradan slaughtering and repenting;
> Nero abandoning his Roman army;
> Jeremiah, writing his Lamentations

all return

in the stories
of the ninth day of Av

and we weep again
at our long history,
our sad history   returning.

Meyer Hahn

SUPERMARKET SHABBAT

You must remember to remember.
But Saturday's child has to work,
and here you are,
chasing carts under the sun
for a market that won't quit,
not for you today, not for them tomorrow.

Spin those wheels, bang those carts.
Let the work roll on:
while the sun dances,
the metal burns,
the market music fills your head.

Now do you remember?
There is a quiet place,
a corner in your mind, candlelit.
All week it was locked tight
like ghetto gates at sundown.
This day it beckons.
You can glimpse the ancient light inside,
settling and settling.

There, beyond all weather,
you may go and refresh yourself.
Will it occur to you?
You would be foolish to forget.

Richard J. Margolis

HAVDALAH

"A good week," we sing
at the end of Shabbat.

"A week as bright as
candlelight, as
sweet as spice
and sweeter than wine!

"A good week!" we sing
as we light the candles
sniff the spice box
and lifting the wine cup
take a sip.

Can you see the light
dancing on your fingertips?

Can you feel inside
another week
ready to begin?

Carol Adler

ACKNOWLEDGMENTS

Grateful acknowledgment is made to the following poets, whose work was especially commissioned for this book:

Carol Adler for "Havdalah." Copyright © 1986 by Carol Adler.

Barbara Juster Esbensen for "The Fourteenth Day of Adar." Copyright © 1986 by Barbara Juster Esbensen.

Meyer Hahn for "Yom ha-Azma'ut" and "Tishah be-Av." Copyright © 1986 by Meyer Hahn.

Kathryn Hellerstein for "Shavuot—for Jessica." Copyright © 1986 by Kathryn Hellerstein.

J. Patrick Lewis for "Dreidl." Copyright © 1986 by J. Patrick Lewis.

Myra Cohn Livingston for "Tu bi-Shevat." Copyright © 1986 by Myra Cohn Livingston.

Richard J. Margolis for "How to Get through the Memorial Service" and "Supermarket Shabbat." Copyright © 1986 by Richard J. Margolis.

R.H. Marks for "Sukkot" and "Simhat Torah." Copyright © 1986 by R.H. Marks.

Harry Philip for "Rosh ha-Shanah Eve." Copyright © 1986 by Harry Philip.

Ruth Roston for "First Night of Hanukkah." Copyright © 1986 by Ruth Roston.

Valerie Worth for "Holy Days." Copyright © 1986 by Valerie Worth Bahlke.

Grateful acknowledgment is also made for the following reprint:

Excerpt from "Passover 1970" from *The Passion of Lizzie Borden: New and Selected Poems* (October House, 1973). Copyright © by Ruth Whitman. Reprinted by permission of the author.